The BIG Snuggle-up

Brian Patten & Nicola Bayley

ANDERSEN PRESS

I asked a scarecrow in out of the snow,
"Please be a guest in my house."
The scarecrow said, "Can I bring a friend,
For in my sleeve lives a mouse?"

Into the house and out of the snow
Came a mouse and an old scarecrow.

A butterfly said, "Is it far too late
For me to come in and hibernate?"

Into the house and out of the snow
Came a butterfly, a mouse, and an old scarecrow.

A robin peeped out from its freezing nest,
"Would you mind if you had another guest?"

Into the house and out of the snow
Came a robin, a butterfly,
a mouse, and an old scarecrow.

A squirrel scampered down from a sycamore tree,
"I'll bring some nuts, if you'll shelter me."

Into the house and out of the snow
Came a squirrel, a robin, a butterfly, a mouse,
and an old scarecrow.

Next a sweet old rabbit with nowhere to go
Begged to be let in out of the snow.

Into the house and out of the snow
Came a rabbit, a squirrel, a robin,
a butterfly, a mouse,
and an old scarecrow.

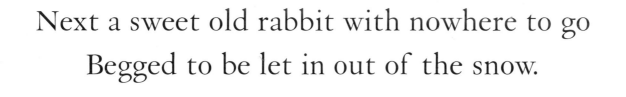

A cat allowed itself to be let in
And it slept on a shelf by a blue bread bin.

Into the house and out of the snow
Came a cat, a rabbit, a squirrel,
a robin, a butterfly, a mouse,
and an old scarecrow.

Next came a dog. It had shaggy hair.
It made itself at home in a comfy chair.

Into the house and out of the snow
Came a dog, a cat, a rabbit, a squirrel,
a robin, a butterfly, a mouse,
and an old scarecrow.

A lamb and a fawn who were lonely and lost
Longed to come in and out of the frost.

Into the house and out of the snow
Came a lamb, a fawn, a dog, a cat, a rabbit,
a squirrel, a robin, a butterfly, a mouse,
and an old scarecrow.

A donkey looked in and said,
"I'm unable
To find my way back and into
the stable."

Into the house and out of the snow
Came a donkey, a lamb, a fawn, a dog, a cat, a rabbit,
a squirrel, a robin, a butterfly, a mouse,
and an old scarecrow.

"The lake," said the heron,
"is covered in ice.
Can I stand in the bath?
It would be nice!"

Into the house and out of the snow
Came a heron, a donkey, a lamb, a fawn, a dog, a cat,
a rabbit, a squirrel, a robin, a butterfly, a mouse,
and an old scarecrow.

Soon into the room sneaked a young fox.
"Can I doze by the fire in a hat-box?"

Into the house and out of the snow
Came a fox, a heron, a donkey, a lamb,
a fawn, a dog, a cat, a rabbit, a squirrel,
a robin, a butterfly, a mouse,
and an old scarecrow.

The owl swooped down silent and slow,
Shaking off flakes of frozen snow.

Into the house and out of the snow
Came an owl, a fox, a heron, a donkey, a lamb,
a fawn, a dog, a cat, a rabbit, a squirrel,
a robin, a butterfly, a mouse,
and an old scarecrow.

And we were all cosy, snuggled up warm
And we listened all night to a terrible storm.

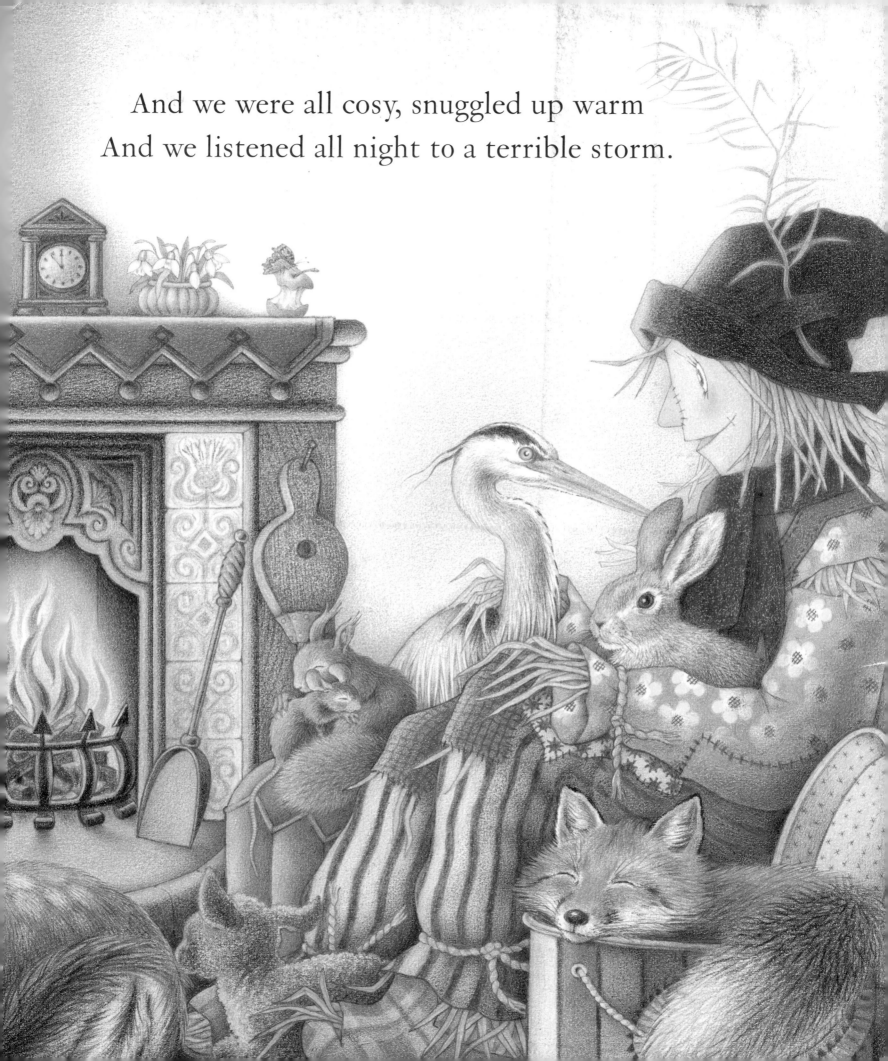

And everyone agreed how nice it would be
To stay in that little warm house with me.